Disney's

THE NEW ADVENTURES OF WINNIE the POOH

Paw and Order

Twin Books

MALLARD PRESS

Kanga and Roo sat in front of a stage in the Hundred-Acre Wood. A play called *Paw and Order* was about to begin.

As the curtains opened, Gopher and Owl sang about the play's hero:

"This hero made an outlaw tame,
And Sheriff Piglet is his name!"

The curtains opened all the way, and Owl and Gopher left the stage. Kanga and Roo could see a blistering-hot desert. A party of hardy pioneers rolled across the dry wasteland in a stagecoach.

"Water! Water!" choked Tigger.

"Honey! Honey!" gasped Winnie the Pooh.

SALOON

At last the pioneers came to Rickety Gulch, a little prairie town. They stopped in front of the saloon. All the townsfolk ran out to warn them.

"Run for your lives!" they yelled. "A gang of horse thieves is comin' to town! We're clearin' out!"

"Oh! Perhaps we should tell the sheriff," suggested Piglet.

"Sheriff!" shouted one of the townsfolk. "We have no sheriff. But *you* can be sheriff!" he said, pinning a badge on Piglet.

"M - m - m - me!" stammered Piglet, shaking nervously.

Just then, a cloud of dust and the thunder of hooves rumbled up Main Street.

"It's the horse thieves!" cried the townsfolk.

Winnie the Pooh and his pals found themselves surrounded by Nasty Jack and his nasty gang.

"I see you have a badge on," snorted Nasty Jack to Piglet. "You must be the sheriff. Me and sheriffs don't get along."

Then Nasty Jack and his gang put Pooh, Piglet, Tigger and Rabbit back in their stagecoach and shoved it down the hill. Pooh and his pals crashed right into the sheriff's office.

As they picked themselves up, they tried to decide what to do.

"I'm getting out of here," said Rabbit, and he ran down the street. But as he passed by the saloon's swinging doors, Nasty Jack grabbed him.

"Howdy, Buckaroo," said Nasty Jack. "You the proprietor of this establishment?"

"N - n - n - no!" stammered Rabbit.

"Then you must be a friend of the sheriff," said Nasty Jack, "and since I hate sheriffs..."

Rabbit knew that if he admitted he was a friend of the sheriff, he'd be in trouble. So he quickly zipped behind the bar to take their orders.

"Banana splits all around!" ordered Nasty Jack. "And pronto!"

As fast as he could, Rabbit made banana splits and served them to Nasty Jack and his gang.

When Nasty Jack got his banana split, he asked, “What? No cherry?”

Nasty Jack grabbed Rabbit by the neck.

“Let me answer that,” coughed Rabbit, “by saying…HELLLLP!”

Pooh, Piglet, Tigger and Eeyore had followed Rabbit and saw what was happening.

"Rabbit's in trouble!" gasped Pooh.

"What should we do, Pooh?" asked Piglet.

"You're the sheriff, Piglet," answered Pooh. "You have to give *us* orders."

"Well, then," said Piglet, "I order you to think of something!"

“I’ve got it!” said Tigger, bouncing with joy. “I’ll go in the front door an’ keep ’em occupied, while Pooh and Eeyore go in the back door an’ rescue ol’ long ears!”

“What’ll *I* do?” asked Piglet.

“You stay here, lookin’ sheriffy,” said Tigger, “and when we’re all set, you give the signal to *go*!”

When everybody was ready, Piglet gave the signal.
"R-r-ready? G-g-go!" shouted Piglet.
Tigger bounced boldly into the saloon.

"Ki-yi whoopeeyay!" sang Tigger. "I'm gonna rope ya, sonny, if ya don't drop that bunny!"

Nasty Jack dropped Rabbit, and watched in disbelief as Tigger twirled his lariat and did all sorts of rope tricks.

Meanwhile, Pooh and Eeyore sneaked in the back door.

But Nasty Jack's gang was ready for them. As soon as Pooh and Eeyore entered the room, some of the horse thieves dropped barrels over them and rolled them right back out into the street.

Other horse thieves tied up Tigger and Rabbit while Nasty Jack grabbed Piglet and plunked him down on the bar.

“Well, sheriff,” sneered Nasty Jack, “it looks like it’s trouncin’ time for you and your pals.”

Suddenly, the swinging doors flew open, and in stomped THE MASKED BEAR, accompanied by his faithful steed.

"Freeze!" said the Masked Bear. "If you please."

With his spurs "ching-ching-chinging" across the floor, the Masked Bear faced Nasty Jack.

"And who are you?" asked Nasty Jack.

"I am the Masked Bear," said the Masked Bear, "and this is my faithful steed."

Slowly, Nasty Jack reached behind the bar and pulled out a huge scoop of strawberry ice cream. Without warning, he flipped the ice cream at the Masked Bear.

The Masked Bear ducked out of the way of the flying ice cream, tripped over his faithful steed, rolled across the floor and crashed into the player piano.

The music roll popped out of the piano, rolled across the floor and hit Nasty Jack in the ankles.

Nasty Jack fell to the floor and rolled right out the door. He landed in the watering trough in front of the saloon. With a splash, a sputter and a spurt, Nasty Jack shook the water out of his face.

While everyone was busy laughing, Piglet was busy cutting the ropes on Rabbit and Tigger. They all escaped back to the sheriff's office.

Nasty Jack and his gang stuffed the Masked Bear and his faithful steed back into barrels and rolled them out the door.

The Masked Bear and his faithful steed rolled down the hill, all the way to the edge of Rickety Gulch Canyon.

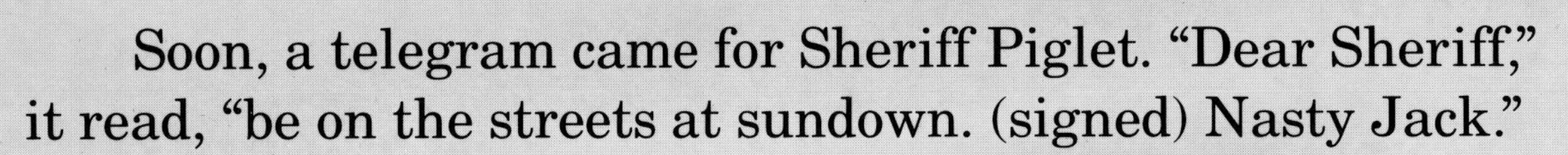

Soon, a telegram came for Sheriff Piglet. “Dear Sheriff,” it read, “be on the streets at sundown. (signed) Nasty Jack.”

“I just remembered,” said Piglet, “I have a very important appointment…heh-heh-heh…under my bed!”

“But, Piglet,” said Tigger, “you *have* to face Nasty Jack! All the townsfolk are depending on you.”

Just then, all the townsfolk, who had been hiding under the floorboards and in the cracks in walls, popped out and cheered, “Yeah!”

“B - b - b - but…well…oh, okay,” said Piglet.

As the late afternoon sun settled on the horizon, the main street was dusty and deserted. Silhouetted against the fading light of day, Nasty Jack stood in the middle of the street, waiting for Sheriff Piglet. Nervously, Piglet stepped into the street to face him.

Piglet was so nervous, every inch of his little body shook like a leaf.

"M - m - Mr. Nasty Jack, sir," sputtered poor Piglet, "as sh - sh - sheriff of this town, I p - p - p - place you under arrest, if you don't mind."

At that moment, because he was shaking so much, Piglet's badge popped off!

"Now look what you did!" snarled Nasty Jack. "Your badge fell off! You know what that means?"

"I'm n - not sheriff anymore?" asked Piglet.

"You're not sheriff anymore!" snorted Nasty Jack. "That's just peachy! Now who am I going to trounce? What am I going to do?"

"Ahh…maybe *you* could be sheriff," suggested Piglet.

"Honest?" asked Nasty Jack, a smile creeping across his face. "Ya mean it? I always *wanted* to be a sheriff!"

Nasty Jack proudly put on the sheriff's badge and turned to his gang of horse thieves. "All right, pilgrims! *I'm* the sheriff now…and I'm *really* gonna clean up this town!" he snarled at them. "UNDERSTAND?"

And with that, all of Nasty Jack's gang high-hoofed it out of town. All the townsfolk cheered as they came out of their hiding places. At last, peace came to Rickety Gulch.

As the sun set on the western horizon, Pooh and Eeyore finally got out of the barrels at the edge of Rickety Gulch Canyon.

"I'm thirsty," said Pooh. "Let's go get a sarsaparilla."

"Lead the way," said Eeyore.

When they got back to the saloon, everyone joined them in a root-beer toast to the new sheriff of Rickety Gulch.

Christopher Robin began to close the curtains.

After the curtains drew shut, Kanga and Roo applauded. Pooh, Piglet, Tigger, Eeyore and Rabbit came through the curtains to take a bow. Owl and Gopher returned to the stage to sing:

"And so the legend has been told
Of Sheriff Piglet, brave and bold.
A hero and a loyal friend,
He gives this tale a happy end."